# WINDY POPS!

## CONTENTS

Cole Day lives in the town of Shiverton with his parents, his sister, Winter, and pet dog, Jeff.

All a bit boring until, one day... **COSSSSHHH!** A stray snowball hit Cole on the back of his head!

But it wasn't just any snowball. It was a RADIOACTIVE snowball! And it turned Cole into Snow-Man – the world's chilliest superhero!

Now, whenever he munches on a raw carrot, Cole's body transforms into a big, white, fluffy man of action!

It's down to Snow-Man and his team, **THIN ICE** and **FROSTBITE**, to defeat the world's nastiest weather-changing villains.

Bad guys, you'd better freeze! SNOW-MAN is slip-sliding your way...

# CAST OF CHARACTERS

Cole

Winter

Jeff

Gail Force

SNOW-MAN

# VOCABULARY

| | |
|---|---|
| disappointed | ingredient |
| hoovering | tornado |
| inflated | whirlwind |

# Chapter One

# Breeze

Cole Day stared unhappily at his breakfast. Whatever was in his bowl didn't look very tasty.

He wasn't even sure what it was. Lumps of purple floated around in a sea of brown… stuff.

His sister, Winter, and their dad didn't like the look of it, either.

"It's my new recipe," said Mum, happily. "Prune Surprise!"

"Why do you call it that?" asked Cole.

"Because it's got prunes in, of course!"

"Yes, but what's the surprise bit?" said Winter.

Mum's eyes twinkled. "The secret ingredient – coffee!"

Cole felt his stomach flip over. "You've given us prunes in coffee for breakfast?" he asked.

"No," Mum said. "I've given you Prune Surprise!"

"Well, I thought it was delicious," said Dad, sliding his empty bowl across the table. "Now I must be off to work." He jumped up and grabbed his coat.

"Yes, I've got to go, too," said Mum, looking at her watch. "I have a special weather report to record this morning. I'll be back in about an hour."

Soon, both parents were hurrying out of the door. Silence fell over the kitchen.

"What did Dad do with his Prune Surprise?" asked Winter.

A loud **BURP** came from under the table. Cole and Winter peeped beneath the tablecloth to see their pet dog, Jeff. He was licking his lips.

"He gave it to Jeff," sighed Cole. "I wish I'd thought of that!"

Jeff **BURPED** again.

"Well, I'm not eating mine!" said Winter, pushing her bowl away.

"Mum will be really disappointed if you don't," said Cole.

Jeff **BURPED**. Really loudly this time.

"Actually," said Cole, "I don't think I'll eat mine either."

"So, what can we do with two bowls of Prune Surprise?" asked Winter.

Suddenly, a huge gust of wind blew the kitchen door open, knocking the children off their chairs and spraying their bowls of Prune Surprise over the wall.

"Well," said Cole, staring up at the mess. "We could always use it to redecorate."

# Chapter Two

# Gust

Cole and Winter climbed to their feet, holding on to the kitchen counter to stop themselves from being blown over again.

All around them plates, food and cutlery were spinning through the air, caught in the powerful wind.

The wind gusted through the kitchen and into the rest of the house, swirling around every room in turn.

"When Mum said she was recording a special weather report, I didn't think she meant this!" shouted Winter.

"That's because it's not really the weather!" yelled Cole. "Look!"

He pointed to the back door where an old lady was standing.

She wore a yellow dress and pink slippers and she was holding what looked like the hose from a very large vacuum cleaner.

"Hello, kiddies!" shrieked the old woman. "My name is **Gail Force**, and I'll be your robber for today!"

"Robber?" cried Cole against the wind. "House destroyer, more like!"

Gail Force laughed. "That's the power of my Superfan!" she bellowed. "Watch what happens when I reverse it..."

The old woman flicked a switch from **BLOW** to **SUCK** and suddenly everything that had been flying around was dragged up inside the pipe.

The microwave oven, the kettle and the toaster.

Items flew in from other rooms, as well. Winter's TV, Dad's laptop, Cole's game console, Jeff's water bowl and more.

It all shot up the hose in **Gail Force**'s hands.

Eventually, she shut the machine off. "Thanks for the pressies!" she shouted. "I must fly!"

Then she raced off down the garden.

Cole, Winter and Jeff stood in what was left of their kitchen.

"Well, at least she didn't suck this up!" said Cole, pulling a raw carrot from his pocket.

Winter smiled.

Jeff **BURPED** again.

# Chapter Three

# Wind

Cole bit off a big lump of carrot and began to chew.

Instantly, a frozen whirlwind blew up from the kitchen floor and wrapped itself around the trio. Icicles flashed, rain showered and snow settled at their feet.

A moment later – exactly where Cole had been – stood a white giant of a figure, dressed in a top hat and red scarf.

He had eyes as black as coal, and what remained of the carrot formed his nose.

This was SNOW-MAN – the world's chilliest superhero!

Standing beside Snow-Man were the two members of his super team – a girl named Thin Ice, and Frostbite, his trusty dog.

Who **BURPED**.

"That stinks, even through a carrot nose!" said Snow-Man, waving his hand to clear the air.

"Never mind that," said Thin Ice, racing for the door.

"Let's get after **Gail Force** before she steals everything in Shiverton!"

The three heroes ran out of the house and down the garden, where they skidded to an icy halt.

**Gail Force** had already blasted into and stolen from the next two houses in the street.

Everything she took was sucked up the hose of her Superfan and stored inside a huge bag on wheels that she dragged along behind her.

Snow-Man shielded his eyes against the winter sun and peered down the street.

"Icicles!" he exclaimed. "**Gail Force** has just got three more houses to go before she reaches…"

"…the *National Bank of Shiverton*!" cried Thin Ice.

"If she blows her way into the vaults, she'll be able to steal everyone's savings!"

"To the Snow-Mobile, let's go!" shouted Snow-Man.

Thin Ice pulled a wooden sledge from her backpack, then both she and Snow-Man jumped aboard.

Frostbite took his place in the reins, and he began to pull the sled – slowly and steadily – towards **Gail Force**.

# Chapter Four

# Hurricane

"Stop right there you hurricane hag!" demanded Snow-Man as Frostbite struggled to drag the Snow-Mobile towards **Gail Force**.

The old woman finished her latest suck and rob attack, then threw back her head and laughed.

"Well, if it isn't Snow-Drop and his soppy sidekicks!"

Snow-Man jumped up and ran the rest of the way down the street.

"I order you to put everything you have stolen back exactly where you found it," he said, pointing to the huge swollen bag of loot.

"No chance, snowball brain!" cackled **Gail Force**, then she turned her Superfan back to **BLOW** and gave our hero a powerful blast of wind.

Snow-Man was lifted up in the air and crashed down on top of his superteam.

Frostbite shook the snow off his fur. "**BARK! WOOF! YIP!**" he said, urgently.

"You're right, boy!" replied Snow-Man. "But we're not going to stop Gail Force before she gets to the bank. We're going to let her rob the place!"

"We are?" cried Thin Ice.

Snow-Man nodded, his top hat bobbling around. "But she won't find just money when she blasts her way into the vault. She'll be met with a chilly reception as well!"

"What do we have to do?" asked Thin Ice.

Snow-Man smiled. "I just need you and Frostbite to distract old windy Wendy over there for about five minutes..."

Gail Force was hoovering up valuable items from the house next to the bank, when her Superfan suddenly stopped working.

Puzzled, the old woman turned to find that Thin Ice had switched off her machine.

"How dare you!" she yelled. "That's my blaster!"

"And this," grinned Thin Ice, "is mine..." Grabbing Frostbite, she squeezed the dog's tummy.

The last of the Prune Surprise gas came gushing out of his mouth in one, huge

# Chapter Five

# Tornado

"Oh, that is disgusting!" cried **Gail Force**, pinching her nose.

"I need some fresh air!" Switching her Superfan back on, she aimed the hose at the two heroes and blew them across to the other side of the street.

Then, she turned her attention to the *National Bank of Shiverton*...

"I've come to clear my account!" she shouted as she blasted her way in through the front doors.
"In fact, I've come to clear everyones accounts!"

The door to the bank's vault crashed inwards from the force of her wind machine.

When she heard it **CLANG** against the ground, she once more flicked the switch beside her from **BLOW** to **SUCK**.

Thousands and thousands of notes were sucked into the hose of the Superfan, along with trays of jewels, priceless documents – and Snow-Man himself!

Our favourite frozen hero had hidden himself inside the bank vault in order to spring his trap.

As he passed **Gail Force**, he reached out and broke off the switch that controlled the machine.

Then he was dragged into the bag of loot.

"What have you done?!" screamed **Gail Force**. "I can't turn it off now – it's stuck on **SUCK!**"

Inside the vast bag, Snow-Man tumbled around in a tornado of items taken from people's homes…

The material creaked as the bag inflated further and
further, until…

It exploded, sending all the stolen goods flying into
the air.

Thankfully, everything landed safely in the deep
snowdrifts at the sides of the road – as did Snow-Man.

Thin Ice and Frostbite raced over to arrest **Gail Force**.

The old woman looked weird – half of her hair had been blasted away when the Superfan exploded.

"Now all we have to do is return all this stuff to the original owners," Thin Ice pointed out.

**Snow-Man** jumped up, chuckling. "Don't worry," he said. "It will be a breeze!"

# QUESTIONS

1. What has Mum made for breakfast? *(page 6)*

2. Who is the only one to eat the breakfast? *(page 8)*

3. Who is blasting in doors and stealing things with her Superfan? *(page 11)*

4. Who pulls the Snow-Mobile? *(page 17)*

5. What is the villain's final target? *(page 17)*

6. Who is inside the machine when it explodes? *(page 28)*

# MEET THE
# AUTHOR AND ILLUSTRATOR

## THE AUTHOR

**Tommy Donbavand** spent his
school days writing stories
in which more popular kids
than him were attacked
and devoured by slavering
monsters. Years later, he's still
doing the same thing – only now
people pay him for it. The fools!

## THE ILLUSTRATOR

**Steve Beckett** has a robot arm
that is programmed to draw
funny pictures. He likes
playing with toy soldiers
and dreams of being an ace
survival expert. He is scared
of heights, creepy crawlies and
doesn't like camping!